D1505970

T2-CPI-271

A RUSSIAN FOLK TALE

PRINCE IVAN AND THE FIREBIRD

Retold and Illustrated by

Laszlo Gal

FIREFLY BOOKS

A FIREFLY BOOK

Cataloguing in Publication Data

Gal, Laszlo
Prince Ivan and the firebird
ISBN 0-920668-98-4

I. Title.

PS8563.A4P75 1991   j398.2′049171   C91-093494-0
PZ8.1.G35Pr 1991

Designed by: Laszlo Gal

Printed and bound in Hong Kong

Published in the United States by:
Firefly Books (U.S.) Inc.,
P.O. Box 1325,
Ellicott Station,
Buffalo, NY
14205

To
the Memory of
Dr. Bruno Nardini

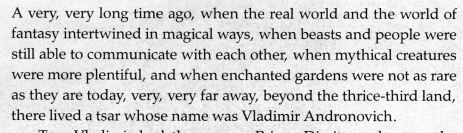

A very, very long time ago, when the real world and the world of fantasy intertwined in magical ways, when beasts and people were still able to communicate with each other, when mythical creatures were more plentiful, and when enchanted gardens were not as rare as they are today, very, very far away, beyond the thrice-third land, there lived a tsar whose name was Vladimir Andronovich.

Tsar Vladimir had three sons: Prince Dimitry, who was the eldest, Prince Vasily, the middle son, and Prince Ivan, the youngest. Tsar Vladimir also had a magnificent garden that was the wonder of all who saw it. It had the most beautiful flowers, and the rarest and most exquisite trees, bearing delicious fruits. The most precious of these was an apple tree that bore fruits of pure gold. The tsar

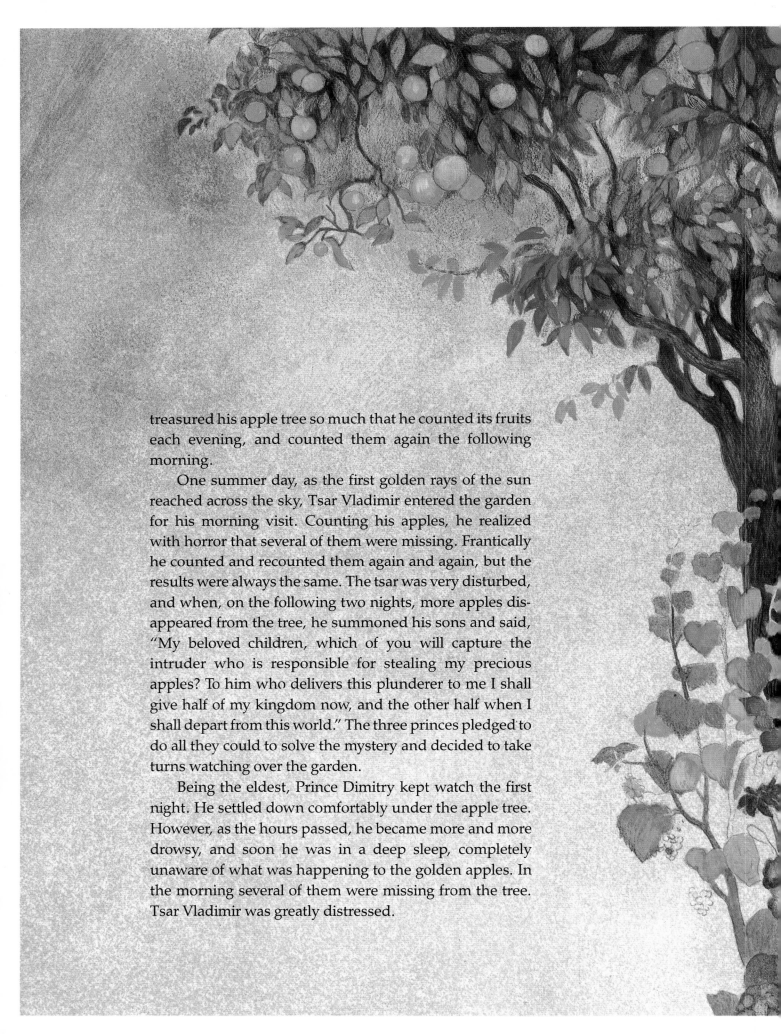

treasured his apple tree so much that he counted its fruits each evening, and counted them again the following morning.

One summer day, as the first golden rays of the sun reached across the sky, Tsar Vladimir entered the garden for his morning visit. Counting his apples, he realized with horror that several of them were missing. Frantically he counted and recounted them again and again, but the results were always the same. The tsar was very disturbed, and when, on the following two nights, more apples disappeared from the tree, he summoned his sons and said, "My beloved children, which of you will capture the intruder who is responsible for stealing my precious apples? To him who delivers this plunderer to me I shall give half of my kingdom now, and the other half when I shall depart from this world." The three princes pledged to do all they could to solve the mystery and decided to take turns watching over the garden.

Being the eldest, Prince Dimitry kept watch the first night. He settled down comfortably under the apple tree. However, as the hours passed, he became more and more drowsy, and soon he was in a deep sleep, completely unaware of what was happening to the golden apples. In the morning several of them were missing from the tree. Tsar Vladimir was greatly distressed.

The second night it was Prince Vasily's turn, but after a few hours he too fell asleep, and by the following morning more golden apples were gone. The tsar was terribly sad.

The third night Prince Ivan took his turn. To keep himself alert he walked around and around the apple tree, counting his steps to pass the time. He walked one hour, then he walked a second hour, then a third. All at once, out of the dark sky he saw a bright light approaching, illuminating everything in its path. The whole garden was flooded with a brilliant golden glow, and the apple tree was so bright that Ivan was unable to look at it. When he finally raised his head he couldn't believe his eyes. Perched on the branch of the tsar's favourite apple tree was a Firebird. Her marvellously bright plumage was golden and her eyes were like precious stones. Quietly, Prince Ivan stole up the tree, climbed the first two branches, and seized her tail, but he could not hold on to her. She tore herself free from his grasp and flew away, leaving the garden in darkness. Prince Ivan was thrown to the ground and remained there stunned, with a feather in his hand from the tail of the beautiful Firebird.

The next morning he went to see Tsar Vladimir in his chambers. He told him what had occurred during the night, and gave him the golden feather. The tsar was so pleased that he placed the feather in a fine jewel-box, to be treasured forever. Day after day the tsar admired this beautiful plume and imagined how magnificent the Firebird must be. During the night he dreamt about it. He also feared for his apples as long as the Firebird remained free. Finally, one morning, he summoned his three sons and said, "My beloved children, go in the name of God and search the four corners of the world. Find the Firebird. To him who brings her back to me alive I shall give as I promised half my kingdom now, and the other half when I die."

Ill will had filled the hearts of the two elder brothers, because Prince Ivan had had more success than they, so they decided to go without him. After putting on their finest armour and choosing the two fastest horses from the stable, they set out together in search of the Firebird.

Prince Ivan, too, put on his armour, picked out a horse, and set out alone to find the Firebird. For many days he travelled in the direction from which the Firebird had appeared that night in the garden. Heavy clouds were almost touching the earth when he arrived at a vast meadow. In this field stood a huge pillar of black granite, and on its surface these words were written:

From this pillar, whoever keeps on going
    straight ahead will be cold and hungry.
Whoever goes to the left will be killed,
    but his horse will stay alive.
Whoever goes to the right will survive,
    but his horse will be killed.

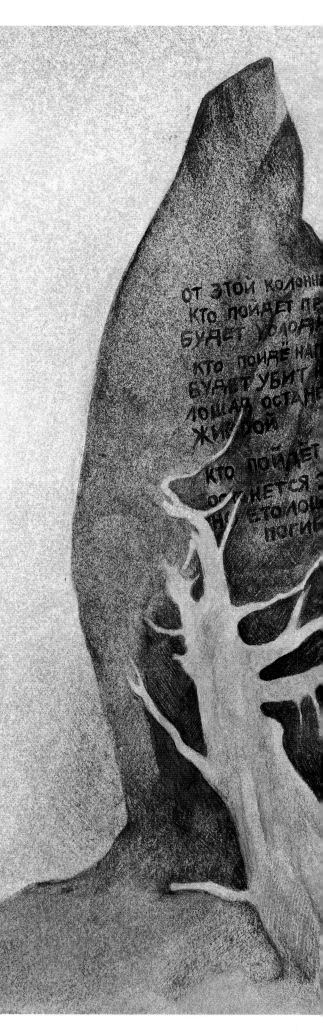

After some thought, Prince Ivan chose to go to the right, and for two days and two nights he rode through an immense dark forest. On the third day, a huge grey wolf leapt from the thicket. It attacked his horse, and killed it, and carried it off into the woods. Frightened and upset, Prince Ivan continued on foot. After a day of walking, he was hungry and utterly exhausted. He was about to sit down and rest a little, when all at once the big grey wolf appeared before him and said, "I am sorry I killed your steed, Prince Ivan, but my friends were starving. I am also sorry that I caused you hardship. Just tell me where you want to go, and I shall take you."

Prince Ivan told him about the Firebird, and about the tree with the golden apples, and about his father, Tsar Vladimir, who sent him to find the Firebird. The grey wolf attended carefully and said: "Listen to me, Prince Ivan. I know where the Firebird can be found, and if you wish, just sit on my back and I will take you there." So the prince got on his back and they darted off more swiftly than birds can fly. They ran through forests and meadows, and over mountains and valleys, until they came to a magnificent palace surrounded by a walled garden. There the wolf stopped and said, "Prince Ivan, climb carefully over the wall. Beyond it, in the garden, you will find the Firebird in a golden cage. Take her, but do not touch the cage, or surely you will be caught at once."

Prince Ivan climbed the wall and carefully took the Firebird out of the cage. He was about to leave the garden, when he decided that the bird would be difficult to carry without the cage to put it in. However, no sooner had he touched the cage than there was a loud sounding of bells, since strings were attached to it. The guards woke up, rushed into the garden, captured Prince Ivan, and led him to their tsar, whose name was Dolmat. The tsar was seated on his throne, and beside him on a table stood a golden chest, full of golden apples. Ivan recognized the apples from his father's garden.

When Tsar Dolmat heard from the guards that this young lad had been about to steal his Firebird, he was furious. In a loud, angry voice he demanded of Prince Ivan, "Who are you? What is your name? Where are you from?"

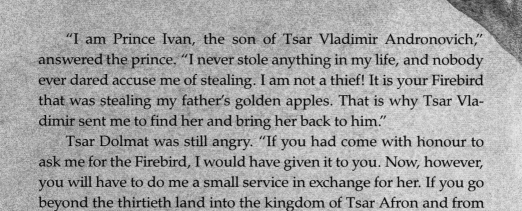

"I am Prince Ivan, the son of Tsar Vladimir Andronovich," answered the prince. "I never stole anything in my life, and nobody ever dared accuse me of stealing. I am not a thief! It is your Firebird that was stealing my father's golden apples. That is why Tsar Vladimir sent me to find her and bring her back to him."

Tsar Dolmat was still angry. "If you had come with honour to ask me for the Firebird, I would have given it to you. Now, however, you will have to do me a small service in exchange for her. If you go beyond the thirtieth land into the kingdom of Tsar Afron and from there bring back to me the horse with the golden mane, I shall give you the Firebird. But if you fail, I will tell everyone throughout all the kingdoms that Prince Ivan is a common thief."

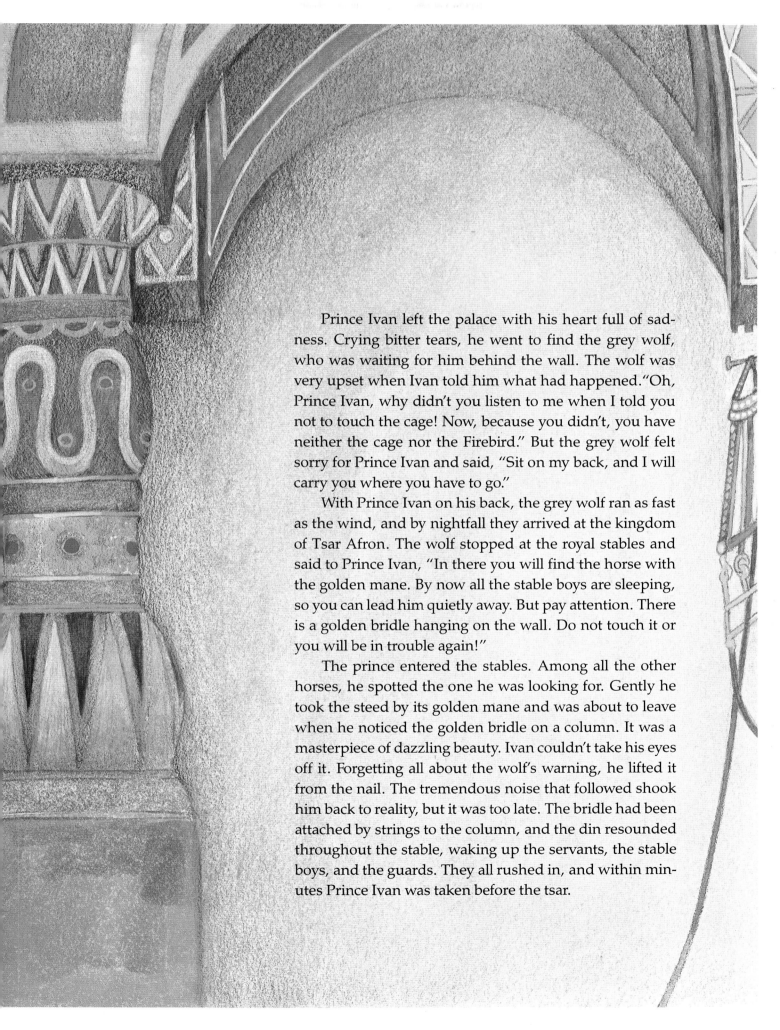

Prince Ivan left the palace with his heart full of sadness. Crying bitter tears, he went to find the grey wolf, who was waiting for him behind the wall. The wolf was very upset when Ivan told him what had happened. "Oh, Prince Ivan, why didn't you listen to me when I told you not to touch the cage! Now, because you didn't, you have neither the cage nor the Firebird." But the grey wolf felt sorry for Prince Ivan and said, "Sit on my back, and I will carry you where you have to go."

With Prince Ivan on his back, the grey wolf ran as fast as the wind, and by nightfall they arrived at the kingdom of Tsar Afron. The wolf stopped at the royal stables and said to Prince Ivan, "In there you will find the horse with the golden mane. By now all the stable boys are sleeping, so you can lead him quietly away. But pay attention. There is a golden bridle hanging on the wall. Do not touch it or you will be in trouble again!"

The prince entered the stables. Among all the other horses, he spotted the one he was looking for. Gently he took the steed by its golden mane and was about to leave when he noticed the golden bridle on a column. It was a masterpiece of dazzling beauty. Ivan couldn't take his eyes off it. Forgetting all about the wolf's warning, he lifted it from the nail. The tremendous noise that followed shook him back to reality, but it was too late. The bridle had been attached by strings to the column, and the din resounded throughout the stable, waking up the servants, the stable boys, and the guards. They all rushed in, and within minutes Prince Ivan was taken before the tsar.

"Well, well, we just caught a young horse thief," said Tsar Afron, and he started to question Ivan. When he heard that the "horse thief" was a prince and that his father was Tsar Vladimir, he said, "Why didn't you ask me honourably for the horse? I would have given it to you with great pleasure. But listen to me, Prince Ivan. If you want me to give you the horse with the golden mane, you will have to do me a great service."

He got up from his throne and came close to Ivan. Ivan noticed that he was very old. His beard was unkempt and dirty, reaching down to his waist. His eyes burned as he talked in a low voice. "Beyond the thrice-ninth land in the thrice-tenth kingdom lives Princess Elena the Fair, whom I love hopelessly with all my heart and all my soul. Go to her kingdom and bring her back to me, and you can have the horse with the golden mane. Should you fail to bring back the princess, I will let everyone know throughout the kingdoms that you are a lowly thief."

Prince Ivan felt miserable and very, very sad. He left the palace with his heart deeply troubled and went to join the grey wolf at the stables. "I warned you about the bridle, didn't I!" said the grey wolf when he heard what had happened to Ivan. "It is the seond time that this has happened to you because you ignored my advice." Knowing very well how right the wolf was, the prince couldn't say a word. He just stood there, speechless.

The grey wolf felt sorry for him and said, "Stop worrying, Prince Ivan. I know where Princess Elena the Fair lives. Just sit on my back and in no time at all we will be there." And so it happened. In a short time they were standing outside the golden fence that surrounded the magnificent palace of Princess Elena the Fair. "Listen to me, Prince Ivan," said the grey wolf. "This time I will go for the Princess myself. Just stay there behind that large oak and wait until I accomplish what we came for."

Late that afternoon Princess Elena the Fair and all her ladies-in-waiting came to the garden for a walk. When the grey wolf saw that she was getting close to his hiding place, he jumped over the fence and seized the princess, who immediately fainted dead away. He put her on his back and ran as fast as the wind to where Prince Ivan was waiting for them.

"Quick, jump on my back or the palace guards will catch up with us!" said the wolf when he reached the prince. Ivan jumped onto his back and took Elena into his arms, and like an arrow the grey wolf darted off with them towards Afron's kingdom.

As Ivan held Princess Elena in his arms he was struck by her great beauty, and he watched her anxiously, waiting for her eyes to open. Finally she awoke and, as soon as she looked up and saw a young and handsome prince embracing her, she fell instantly in love with him, as he did with her.

Now the thought of handing Princess Elena over to Tsar Afron tormented Ivan's soul, and when they reached Afron's palace his heart overflowed with sadness and he wept bitterly.

"Why are you crying, Prince Ivan?" asked the wolf.

"Oh, grey wolf! I love Elena with all my heart. How can I give her to Tsar Afron?" Ivan moaned.

"Well Prince, I have been a friend of yours and have served you well. I will help you again. Because I can alter my appearance, I will turn myself into Princess Elena. Instead of the real princess, you will escort me to the tsar. When he gives you the horse with the golden mane, take the real princess and ride as fast as you can, as far as possible, and leave the rest to me."

Saying this, the grey wolf rolled over and, in an instant, he had turned into Elena the Fair. Then, Prince Ivan called on the tsar with the false princess.

When Tsar Afron saw the princess he had dreamed about all these years, he rejoiced, and happily gave the horse to Prince Ivan in exchange. Prince Ivan was happy too. He mounted the steed and galloped through the palace gate to meet his beloved Elena. He seated her behind him, and together they set out towards the kingdom of Tsar Dolmat.

For three days, as they travelled through valleys and mountains, the grey wolf, disguised as Elena the Fair, lived in the palace of Tsar Afron. On the fourth day he went to the tsar and said, "My Lord, let me take a walk in the green meadows to dispel this great sadness from my soul!"

When Tsar Afron heard that his beloved Elena was sad, he ordered all the governesses and nurses and all the ladies-in-waiting to go for a walk with the princess. The whole party strolled out through the green meadow, and when nobody was paying attention, the grey wolf slipped away into an area that was covered with thick foliage. There he transformed himself back to his original form. There was a terrible confusion amongst the servants as the big wolf jumped out of the dense bush, and great panic when they realized that the princess had vanished from sight.

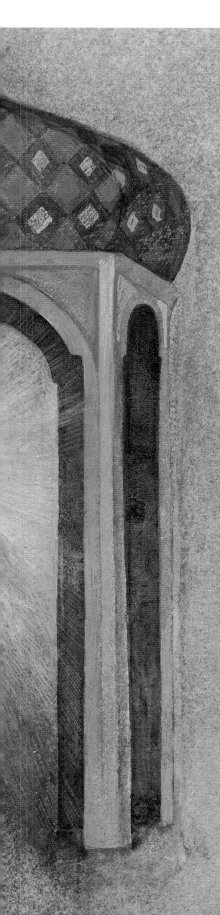

A short time later, Prince Ivan and Princess Elena were riding along a forest path when, all of a sudden, the grey wolf stood before them. "Sit on my back, Prince Ivan, and leave the horse for the princess," said the wolf. So they travelled on like this, Princess Elena on the horse and Prince Ivan on the back of the wolf. During all this time Ivan was very quiet. At long last they neared the kingdom of Tsar Dolmat, and when the palace came into full view before them, they stopped.

Prince Ivan finally broke the silence. Turning to the wolf, he said, "All the golden apples that the Firebird stole from my father were in a golden chest right next to the throne of Tsar Dolmat. I believe I should get even with him. You have been a real friend and have done many a great service for me. Please do me this last one: Change yourself into the horse with the golden mane. I will hand you over to the tsar and keep the real horse for myself."

The grey wolf said nothing. He just rolled over on his back and assumed the shape of the horse with the golden mane. Prince Ivan was delighted, and jumped on the wolf's back. He waved farewell to Princess Elena, telling her to wait for his return, and dashed away in the direction of Tsar Dolmat's palace.

Tsar Dolmat was standing at the window when Prince Ivan galloped through the main gate. The tsar was so overjoyed to see the horse with the golden mane that he ran down the long stairs to greet Prince Ivan in the courtyard. There he took the horse's reins and ushered Prince Ivan into the garden, where the Firebird was locked up in her beautiful golden cage.

"The Firebird is yours, Prince Ivan. Take her," said Tsar Dolmat. Then he invited the prince to stay for a few days.

"Thank you for your welcome, noble tsar, but I still have a long way to go before I reach my homeland," replied Ivan. Then he took the cage with the Firebird and left. Outside the town he mounted the horse with the golden mane, seated Princess Elena behind him, and together they set out for his father's kingdom.

Tsar Dolmat was so eager to try his new horse that at sunrise the next morning he entered the stables and saddled it. However, as soon as he had galloped it out of the palace grounds, the beast became so fierce and wild that Tsar Dolmat found himself flying head first into the thicket, while the horse bolted and disappeared. When he was out of sight, the wolf changed back to his real form and sped away to join Prince Ivan and Princess Elena. He caught up with them at the same place where, days earlier, he had killed Ivan's horse.

"Well, Prince, this is the spot where we first met," he said. "I have served you all this time, but from now on you won't need me. I am not your servant any more, but I am still a friend. Farewell, and God be with you." Having said that, he walked slowly into the dense forest, which seemed to swallow him at once. Prince Ivan and the Princess looked on as the grey wolf vanished amid the gigantic dark trees. They both wept. Then Prince Ivan turned the horse towards his native land, and spurred him gently, and they resumed their homeward journey.

After a long, arduous ride, with the sun blazing high above them, they both felt fatigued. So Prince Ivan reined in the horse, tied it to a large tree, and hung the Firebird in its cage on one of the branches. Then the two lovers lay down in the cool shadow of the tree, and in no time at all they fell asleep.

It so happened that just then, at that same place, the two brothers of Prince Ivan were passing by on their way home from their travels through many kingdoms. Their search for the Firebird had ended in disappointment and bitterness. But then, unexpectedly, in full view a few metres away from them, was the Firebird. Utterly bewildered, they jumped off their horses and rushed towards the cage. As they got closer they saw the two sleeping figures, and with

astonishment they recognized their young brother Ivan. Startled, they stepped behind the tree. Without exchanging words, the two evil souls knew, just by looking at each other, that they both wanted the Firebird for themselves. They also hated Prince Ivan for succeeding so often where they had failed. So they drew lots, and Prince Dimitry pulled the shorter straw. Stepping forward, he plunged his sword into Prince Ivan's heart. Then they woke up Princess Elena. When she saw the slain prince beside her she was horror-stricken, and froze into a terrified silence.

"Listen lovely maiden," said Prince Dimitry. "Now you are in our hands. Tomorrow when you meet our father, you must tell him that Prince Vasily and I captured you, and we captured the horse

and the Firebird as well. And if you want to stay alive, he must not know the fate of Prince Ivan."

Then they divided the spoils between themselves. Prince Dimitry got Elena the Fair, while the horse went to Prince Vasily. Thus they resumed their travels, leaving Prince Ivan's body for the wild animals.

There was great jubilation upon their arrival at their father's palace, and the celebrations lasted seven days. Princess Elena silently agreed to marry Prince Dimitry. The date for the wedding was set for the next full moon.

For ten days Prince Ivan lay dead under the tree. During all that time, a raven, sitting on the branches, kept watch over his dead body, waiting for the right moment to swoop down. On the tenth day, suddenly a voice called out from the edge of the forest, "Don't touch the Prince, raven!" The grey wolf stepped from between the trees. From far away, he had sensed that his friend was in need of help, and knew that he had to hurry back to this place at once if he wanted to save him.

He said to the raven, "Remember when I fed your starving children with the flesh of the horse I killed a while ago? That horse belonged to this young knight. Now he needs your help. Fly beyond the thrice-ninth land and bring me the water of life, and I will be forever grateful to you."

"Very well, I will do this service for you," said the raven, whereupon he took to the air and was soon out of sight.

For three days the grey wolf sat beside Prince Ivan's body, guarding it from the beasts. On the third day the raven came back carrying in his beak a small glass bottle, which was filled with the water of life. The grey wolf took the vial and sprinkled Prince Ivan's body with the water. As soon as the droplets touched his skin, he opened his eyes.

"Ah, why did I sleep so long?" said the prince, looking around, searching for Elena the Fair. Instead he saw the grey wolf.

"You would have slept forever," answered the wolf, "had it not been for the water of life." Then he explained how Ivan's brothers had murdered him and taken Elena the Fair, the horse, and the Firebird, and how the raven fetched the water of life that brought him back from the dead.

"But now we must hurry, because today your brother Dimitry is to marry Elena the Fair." So Ivan sat on the wolf's back, and in a very short time they reached the capital of his father's kingdom. Before entering the town, Ivan dismounted from the grey wolf. Then he

walked the rest of the distance to the palace, ran up the long stair-case, and opened the huge door of the Great Hall, where the wed-ding celebrations had already started. When Elena the Fair saw Prince Ivan enter the hall, she jumped up from her seat and ran directly into his arms.

"This is my true love!" she cried, and then, pointing at Dimitry, she said, "Not that evil soul."

The tsar and all the guests were stunned.

"What is the meaning of all this!?" said Tsar Vladimir, com-pletely confused, not knowing whether to be angry at the distur-bance or happy to see his youngest son return home.

Then Elena the Fair revealed the truth about Ivan's murder, her abduction, and everything else that had happened. The tsar became so furious that he ordered both Dimitry and Vasily to be thrown into the darkest dungeon.

Prince Ivan and Princess Elena were married right then and there, and they all resumed the celebrations. When all the merry-making ended three weeks later, Prince Ivan gave orders for the release of his two brothers, and appointed them to be ambassadors to the kingdoms of Tsar Afron and Tsar Dolmat.

The grey wolf remained a true friend and became the guardian to the Princess and the adviser to the new ruler of half the kingdom, who by now was called Tsar Ivan Andronovich.